By **Lorna Robinson**
Illustrations by **Lydia Hall**

Telling Tales in Nature Forest Tales © Lorna Robinson 2022

All rights reserved. No part of this publication may be reproduced, stored in a retrieval system, or transmitted in any form or by any means, electronic, mechanical, photocopying, recording or otherwise, without the prior written permission of the author.

ISBN: 9798367880434

For my forest girl and our secret wood

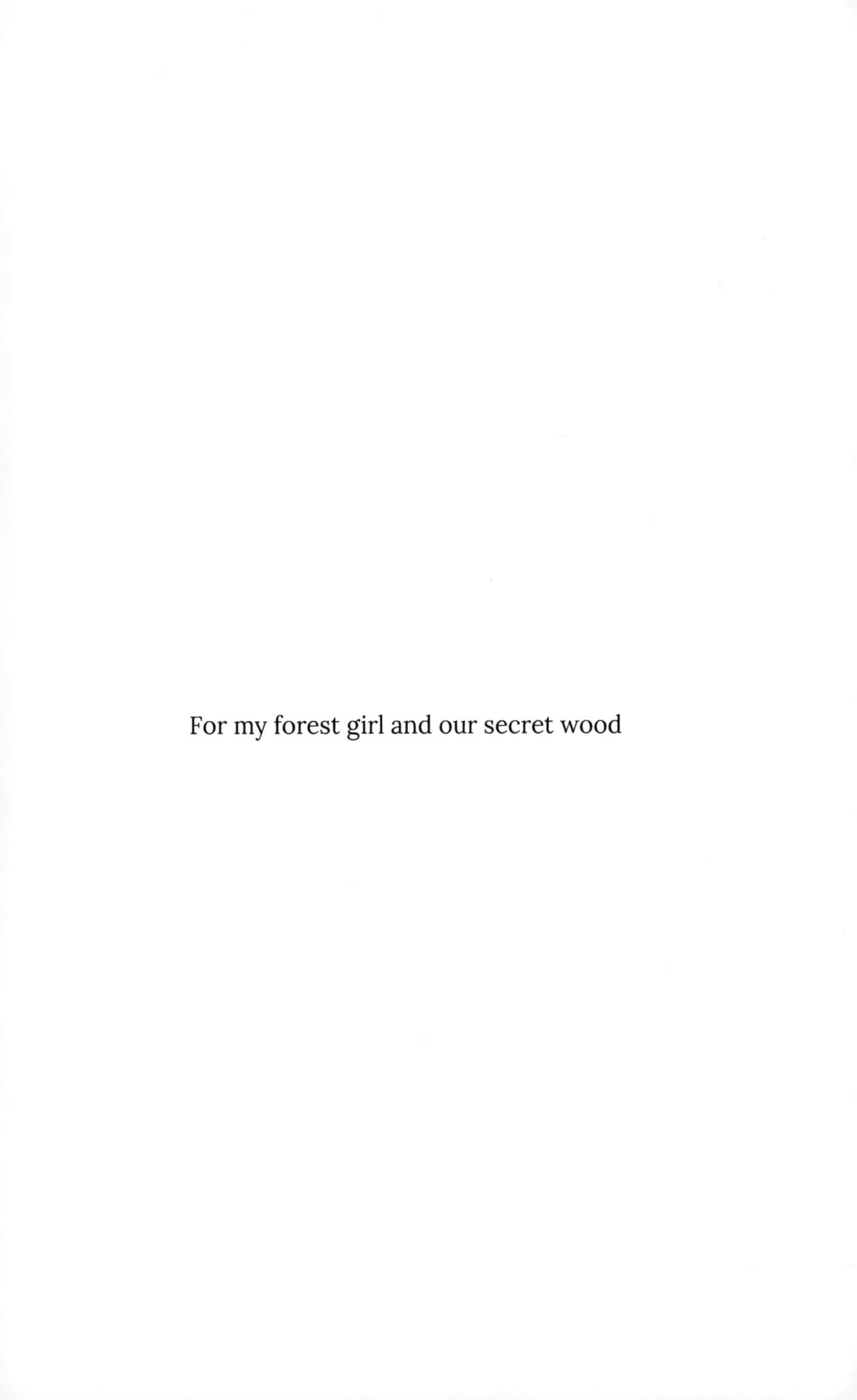

Contents

Introduction 1

Walnut Tree 2

Walnut's Tale 5

Elm Tree 16

The Elm's Tale 19

Holm Oak Tree 27

The Holm Oak's Tale 30

Black Poplar Tree 39

Black Poplar's Tale 41

Introduction

Underworld Tales explored plants associated with that gloomy abode of the dead, and the stories were all connected by their setting: the twilit world underneath ours where ghostly versions of people are bound to drift and roam.

In this second book of the *Telling Tales in Nature* series, the stories are all set in forests in the upper world. They are also all stories of trees, and these particular trees are named in ancient sources as "hamadryad" sisters, that is, nymphs whose lives are bound to their trees. If the tree dies, then the nymph dies with their tree.

There are eight of these sisters in total. In *Forest Tales*, you will meet four of the sisters; the other four will tell their tales another time.

As with the first book in the series, each chapter has an introduction on the plant, with botanical drawing, followed by a retelling of the myth of the tree. It finishes with some brief notes on the sources for the myths and explanations of the retellings.

Step inside our forest and meet the first of the tree sisters...

Walnut Tree

Sitting under a walnut tree on a sun-filled summer day is one of life's joys. The dappled patterns made by the leaves, the green shells of the nuts hanging abundantly overhead, and the scuttling of squirrels up and down its widely outstretched branches. The sense of a future suspended feast is all around!

Walnut trees love the sun, and as well as being sun-loving, these trees are resilient to rainless spells. Their nuts (technically drupes since they are not a 'true' nut - more on these later) secrete a substance that repels other plants from growing nearby, making them a surprisingly powerful tree.

The walnut tree is known as "juglans regia" which means "royal nut of Jupiter". There are various theories about this. One idea is that in the mythological golden age of mankind, men ate acorns and gods ate walnuts, but ancient sources are silent on the matter. The ancient Greek word "karya" can mean a walnut, hazelnut or sweet chestnut, so the story in this chapter, though commonly assumed to refer to walnut, could be any of the three.

Some sources state that walnuts were introduced to Greece as a gift from Persian kings. This is why the Greeks called the walnut "karya basilica," or "royal nut."

The walnuts the tree produces in abundance are encased in tough green shells, which become ready for eating in the autumn. The four seeds inside the shell look a lot like a brain, with the channels and bobbly shapes. These nuts have long been used in the cuisine of many cultures in all sorts of ways, being a rich, buttery nut. Sprinkled on salads, in sauces, pickled, sweetened in desserts, there are all sorts of ways they continue to be enjoyed.

It is not just the nuts that bring delight. Walnut wood has a lovely, deep grainy texture and it is often used for making furniture and musical instruments. Other creatures love the walnut tree too. Lots of different moths live on walnut trees from the walnut sphinx to the beautiful common emerald.

The Greeks and Romans used their leaves to dye their hair. They also used the leaves for anything which caused swelling of the skin, such as ulcers and spots.

There are many stories and songs about the walnut tree. A walnut tree features in a fable of Aesop's, where it laments the ingratitude of those who throw sticks and stones to bring down its fruit. The tale featured here is of the walnut nymph who was once one of three sisters.

FOREST TALES

fig 1.

Juglans Regia

(WALNUT TREE)

fig 2.

Walnut's Tale

Our little village has always had walnut trees. Lots of them, in gardens, lining the market place, at the edges where the tracks wove their way into the horizon. I loved to watch the squirrels running up and down their branches, the green nutcases and leaves rustling, shaking and often falling with a soft thump on the ground. It used to be that the nuts were all gone before we noticed, but these days, now that I'm in charge, I'm careful. Those bushy tailed shadows don't always scurry away with my fruit so easily.

Of course, because walnuts were everywhere, we got used to eating them a lot. My mother loved to use them in all sorts of ways, but her favourite was walnuts and honey, a treat she would leave out for me and my sisters sometimes when we came back from washing clothes in the river. Washing clothes was hard work - all that wringing and carrying the damp heavy material home - we would always argue over who was carrying the most, and when we got back, there would be those higgledy nuts, with all their bumps and curves, dripping in gleaming honey. That usually put an end to our squabble, as we would sit munching and grinning, licking the sweet honey from the edges of our lips and our fingers like small children.

I remember the day a visitor came, and my mother had cooked a special walnut dish. She spent ages preparing it - I could smell the walnuts roasting deliciously, as my sisters and I prepared our very best plates. We were arguing as usual, but it was a friendly argument over who had played the best game last night.

We lived in a palace, though that's now rather a grand word for what it actually was, but as daughters of the King, we lived in relative luxury for our time. We didn't have slaves who did all our cooking and washing and weaving like others may have done, so we regarded ourselves as quite ordinary. But our home was big enough to have bedrooms for each of us, a large women's area of the palace, a kitchen with a stove, and a spacious dining area with outside space. And of course, a little orchard of walnut trees.

"Who is coming? Tell us, please!" we begged our mother while she prepared, but she shook her head at us. She didn't like the airs and graces of those who considered themselves more important than others. "All people should be treated the same in our home, so you don't need to worry about who it is" she told us whenever we wanted to know who our guests were. But we knew enough about the world and the gossip in our little village to know that the people who passed our threshold were often considered very important.

It was the evening when this particular visitor arrived. An ordinary early summer's evening. The air was warm and gentle, and the sky a mellow shade of orange. My sisters and I were sat in the shade of the largest walnut tree, watching, waiting, laughing amongst ourselves about something inconsequential, when he walked up. He was a young, shy-looking man who looked at us carefully as he approached the house, as if we were predators.

It was the usual boring sort of dinner. I don't remember much of it. The familiar clinking of plates and polite conversation which I didn't pay much attention to. The visitor spoke in a low tone to my parents' polite questions. He sometimes smiled, but mostly I remembered him that night as serious and a bit unsure of himself and his surroundings. He left the next morning while we were out at the river, watching the waters dazzle in the sunshine.

I didn't think anything of it until a few months later, he returned. Guests don't usually return that quickly. I wondered what he wanted. "Who do you think he is?" I said to my sister Orphe. She shrugged. "No idea," she said, and carried on chewing a walnut leaf.

The answer to that came in a very big way when our parents invited us all into the room that evening. Our mother and father were stood looking surprised and a bit unsure themselves, and the visitor looked different.

He was the same man, but I saw something different about him. He looked straight at me and in his dark brown eyes I glimpsed something I had never seen before. A brightness and wildness that shook me inside. I stared at those eyes, barely listening to what he was saying, which is unfortunate, as what he was saying would change our lives.

"In honour and thanks for your kind hospitality, I am giving your three daughters a gift. From now on, they will be able to see the future."

The future. Just like that. We smiled, nodded and filed out of the room before heading straight to the walnut tree to talk excitedly.

"What does he mean?"

"Do you see anything about the future?"

"Not a thing! Maybe he was making it all up".

"Strange thing to say, though, yes?"

Our lives continued relatively as normal. But we did start to notice the changes. The future didn't come to us in dreams or in any sort of way that was as clear as that, not that dreams are ever particularly clear. It was more like that sense of what direction things were going to take became stronger than it was before. In later stories, they talked about us having the gift of prophecy but it never felt as powerful as it sounded.

And I got that sense when the visitor approached me the next morning. My sisters were not around, and I was sitting under the tree weaving pieces of grass together.

"What is your name?" he said in his low voice. I looked up at those wild brown eyes and felt a shiver go through me. "Karya," I said.

I don't need to tell the rest, and besides it all happened so quickly, that it felt like only moments later that he was gone, and I was sat on the grass, my body beaded with sweat and my face flushed with excitement and disbelief.

My sisters appeared shortly after, but they didn't notice anything that time. It was after the third or fourth visit that they began to ask questions.

"Sister, where were you this morning?" said Lyco.

"Nowhere much," I replied.

"But you weren't under the tree. Were you at the river? Someone said they saw you there."

I didn't like lying, so eventually I came clean. "Don't tell mother or father", I said anxiously. I knew this was not the sort of behaviour that would be looked upon well. It would bring great shame on the household, a shame that would be carried by me through my lifetime. I knew it was reckless and selfish, but something so powerful lay in that quiet man with his intense eyes.

Months went by, and my life felt no longer my own. Gone were the daily pleasures of time with my sisters, of washing our clothes in the river, of the smell of the walnuts when my mother was cooking them. All I could think of was when he would return. It might have felt a poor exchange for a few hours of pleasure, but it became an addiction, an obsession and nothing else mattered to me anymore.

I woke up on the morning when everything changed to find my sisters in my room, watching me, waiting for me to wake. The sunshine was making patterns through the leaves outside my window, and I remember noticing the patterns seemed to be winking at me that day.

"What are you doing here?" I asked, a little unnerved. Were mother or father unwell, I wondered. "We are taking you somewhere", Orphe said. Their faces told me that questions at this point were not going to be answered, so I went with them. I noticed they had packed bags, but I didn't ask what was in them. I was still a bit sleepy and that sense of what might happen was unsettled, but most definitely bad.

We walked far along the shining river, further than I had ever gone before. "I'm tired!", I said. "Can we stop and rest?" My sisters kept on, one behind and one ahead of me, so I carried on too. Complaining took up too much energy. The sun must have been reaching its peak, when we came to the edges of a wood. Stepping inside, the shade was gentle and cool, and we all felt relieved. We sat down, and my sisters opened one of the bags, which contained a large leather sack filled with water, and some bread. After we were all refreshed from the long journey, I asked "so why have we come all this way?"

"To protect you from yourself, sister". I stared at them, and realised straightaway what had happened. It was like a bolt of lightning to my heart, and I leapt up in panic. The idea of missing him, of missing that dose of wild joy, and being left only with more empty months in between, was unbearable. They grabbed me and pulled me down with a bump.

"You cannot see him, you are ruining your reputation. You know nothing about this man."

"Our parents welcomed him twice to our home, and he bestowed on us a parting gift".

"That's because he is a god. He is Dionysus, god of all that is wild and irresponsible."

I was stunned. I sat in shock, letting the name resonate inside my head. Dionysus. Dionysus. I didn't want to admit it, but it all made sense. The power he held over me, the way my parents had looked after him, the fear in my sisters' eyes. But was it just fear? I thought it was then, but these days I have much time to think, and I wonder now if there was something else there, a trace of triumph, of jealousy, of sisterly resentment at having been the one chosen by this man who is a god.

We stayed in that wood for a day and a night, but this is a god after all. He knew how to find us, and he knew he had been tricked. He appeared, leaning on one of the trees, looking down at us as we looked up at him, all afraid, clinging then to each other. I felt something hit my head with a soft thud and saw it roll down to the floor. It was a walnut. We were sitting under a walnut tree.

What then followed is wiped from my memory or perhaps just happened instantaneously. My sisters became stone statues, holding up buildings, all these centuries, unable to move or to hide anyone or to speak what they feel ever again. The wave of their peploi and the look in their eyes remains.

And me? I became a walnut tree, growing the nuts I used to enjoy eating so much, watching them fall to the ground or get taken by small creatures right off my branches. He comes back to see me sometimes, with those wild brown eyes, and he might pick some of the nuts on the ground if it is the right time of year. The addiction has gone, my heart feels too full of woody veins.

Notes

The story of Karya, the nymph who had a secret affair with Dionysus, god of wine, was recorded by Servius, the fourth century commentator, when writing about the Roman poet Virgil's *Eclogue* XIII.

In the original story, Karya's parents were King Dion of Laconia, and Amphithea. They hosted Apollo, and in return, he granted their three daughters the gift of prophecy. Though, as with most gifts from the gods, this favour came with conditions. The sisters were not allowed to betray the gods. When Dionysus visited, and was hosted with equal warmth by their parents, he fell in love with one of the sisters, Karya. Her two sisters hid Karya when they realised what was going on. In doing so, they were said to have broken the restriction Apollo had given them. Dionysus hunted them and turned them into rocks. Karya herself turned into a walnut tree.

This story forms the foundational story for the cult of Artemis Carytis, priestesses who worshipped Artemis, the goddess, as protector of the nut tree. The beautiful stone caryatids which can be found on the Parthenon are walnut nymphs, stony versions from these stories, supporting their buildings.

I wrote this story from the perspective of Karya herself, to give some light to the darker parts of the story: why did the sisters do what they did? I changed the story so that Dionysus is the only visitor mentioned, and the one who bestows the gift of prophecy.

Elm Tree

The beautiful wych elm tree ("ulmus glabra") is now rare here in Britain after most of these trees were wiped out by Dutch Elm disease, but there are still beautiful examples about, especially further north. It's also known as the Scots Elm, and the famous Loch Lomond is actually a corrupted version of the name *Leamhán* meaning elm in Scots Gaelic.

They are towering and striking trees, growing up to thirty metres tall, and with greyish brown bark which is "fissured", which means it has large ridges in it that run elegantly up its trunks. It has jagged, toothy leaves which are asymmetrical, a lovely oval shape and deep green colour.

The word "wych" means supple or pliant and is connected to the word "wicker".

These trees like the sort of rich soil in river valleys, and unsurprisingly, therefore, wych elms do not do well in drought conditions. It has a lovely grainy pattern to its wood, and is therefore much used in craft to make all sorts of things.

The caterpillars of the White-letter streak butterfly feed on elm leaves, and as a result of the tree's decline in Britain, these butterflies have also become very rare. This butterfly looks like it has a W slashed in white over its pale brown wings, which seems almost to tie it to the wych elm.

This is reminiscent of the hamadryads around which these stories are based - beings that are intrinsically tied to a part of nature.

Their winged fruits are called "samaras", and are dispersed by the wind to create new elms.

They appear in various places in ancient Greek and Roman literature. The great hero Achilles clings to one in the *Iliad*, when the river Scamander rises up against him after getting clogged with the corpses of Trojans. The Roman poet Ovid talks about how the "elm loves the vine, and the vine does not desert the elm", referring to the way that these two plants often coexisted.

Elm tree leaves are amongst the largest of British trees, which relates to our story, told by the hamadryad of the elm tree which sheltered dreams under its leaves, and can be found close to the gates of Hades...

The Elm's Tale

I stand right at the edge of the forest, my mighty old branches throwing their arms far and high, with their large oval leaves. I am the only elm in the forest, and I am proud of my height and my strength. I've been here the longest too, or at least I think I have. So many centuries have I looked one way through the dense woodland on one side of me.

To the other side is something quite different. Tall, dark gates. I don't like to think of what lies beyond those gates. They are higher than my highest branches, and I have not strained to grow any higher, as I do not really want to see the things I have heard of. I know enough from the ghostly faces that make their way to the gates and wait for them to open.

Sometimes, though, over the high walls, come a flock of black-winged birds, moving in spectacular harmony in the way birds do. Their wings beat against the windless air here and they glide in under my leaves. They are not just birds. They are the oneiri, and each one is the bearer of a dream intended for a sleeping mortal. Nymphs like me don't usually dream, but when this flock arrives, I feel the dreams, different each time. Sometimes I forget them quite quickly, but other times they stay with me.

Over the long years I have spread my branches next to that gate for the dreams to dive into and nestle under for a while, one dream has haunted me the most. I can't remember how long ago this one was, but I remember what the dream had to tell me so vividly. It started with a young man.

The young man appeared walking through the forest, past the watchful trees, in the early twilight. His eyes are bright and sad. As he walks, he sings a tune that floats through the trees like the gentlest of bird songs, and behind him, little birds flutter anxiously, squirrels and foxes of the wood appear and run gently behind him, and the branches of the trees themselves seem to lean towards him.

He reaches the end of the forest, where I myself stand. He stops that gentle singing, and looks across at the dark gates. After a few moments, he steps forward, but this time nothing living follows him. They all pause at the threshold of the woods, in the safe shelter of our green branches, the little birds, the small creatures watch him as he moves across that bleak space that lies between our forest and the gates, that living body and soul heading straight for the gates of death.

The thick, sludgy waters of the Styx are waiting for him, reeking of the emptiness that life leaves behind. The boatman would never have accepted a living body, so he dove straight into those waters.

Often in dreams, this is exactly the bit where you get stuck, trying over and over to get through some waves. But this was a very unusual dream, I discovered, as I followed its journey through my leaves and branches. The man swam through those horrible waters without much problem. Even when he reached the monster with the three heads and six fiery red eyes, I did not feel fear in that man's heart in this dream. He sang another song - a different one from the forest song he sang. This one had a peculiar rhythm, almost like a dance.

Those three heads listened, inquisitively, as confused and mesmerised by the strange rhythm as me, and as they listened, the man stepped over rocks and pebbles on that lifeless shore, and walked down the path ahead. He did not stop singing until they were out of sight, and by that time, he was surrounded by a thick mist.

The mist was full of all the ghosts who lived in that desolate place. He could not see their faces or hear their voices, but he could sense their presence all around him, like a song he had never heard before. He was captivated, standing there surrounded in that mist of souls.

He remembered that he had come to that place for a reason, but the reason was fuzzy in the dream. The song of souls had submerged him and he no longer wanted to be anywhere else. The last thing I remember in the dream was that sense of joy of finding the place you belong. I could feel that deep comfort through all the sap in my bark, and all the leaves in my tree.

Like all dreams, this one roosted only a short while, before it flew on its way.

The dream haunted me because I had seen that man when he passed me on his way to those grim gates. I remember him standing for a moment, just like in the dream, looking out with eyes bright with determination, and something else - some emotion that I couldn't read. I can't recall if there was a crowd of creatures following him, but I do remember him standing there, lyre strung over his shoulder, staring ahead of him.

I did not know until long afterward what his mission was. All I knew was that a young, living man with a beautiful voice was heading into the land of the dead. I thought he would get turned away at the first hurdle. It is rare, but not the first time people have headed down to see if they can bring back a loved one from the dead.

Some time later, he returned. I saw him from a distance, almost limping across the empty land that lay between the gate and our forest. I could see that something had been lost, and that his mission had failed. Stories that came many years later filled in the gaps: he had come for his young wife, bitten by a snake hidden in the grass. He had a mournful name: Orpheus. As he walked by me, he paused and looked up. Perhaps he sensed the dreams underneath my leaves, since there were a few at the time.

I saw his eyes bereft and broken. He was not singing now. Then he was on his way along the forest track, visible for a while as a thin, half limping figure, who no longer even looked alive against the deep green of the wood.

It was years later that the dream came to me, and I realised it was his. And I also realised that he had not gone down to that kingdom for love. And that when he returned, his grief was not over his lost wife - I could have told him they would never let her go - but over something else, something he had found while there, that he didn't want to leave behind. The music of old souls perhaps.

Over these centuries so many dreams have flocked under my leaves, and I have grown weary and drained at times from their stories, the worlds they reveal and the suffering and joy they carry with them. The king of dreams himself, Morpheus, has once or twice come to visit me. It was once when a dream didn't wake up from under my leaves. The dream itself was unremarkable, I don't even remember what tale it told, only that it was an unhappy one. But after several days, after its flock had headed back over those high gates, that dream remained.

Morpheus appeared not long after, walking through the woodland in his long coat, the colour of twilight. It trailed on the ground, and behind him, a strange atmosphere descended. Hazy, dreamy, hypnotically slow.

As he approached, I saw his face, pale and bright and empty as the moon. He reached a hand up into the branch where the dream lay sleeping, and took the creature in his slender hand. I saw his long coat was now constantly shifting its colour to different shades of twilight. I felt all the sensation and emotion from the dream drain out from my branches, and I felt relieved.

Morpheus set off towards the high gates with the dream, and then they were both gone. I waited until the next time a cluster of dreams flew over the wall and headed my way, and my tree was full again.

Notes

Homer tells of the Oneiri in his *Odyssey*, where he describes them as residing in the shores of Oceanus in the west, and emerging to sleepers through gates: one of ivory (where deceiving dreams come through) and one of horn (for 'true' dreams). Hesiod, the ancient Greek poet from roughly the same time period, also mentions the dreams, saying that their mother is Nyx.

Morpheus is imagined vividly by the Roman poet Ovid in his *Metamorphoses*, where he describes him as one of the sons of sleep, winging his way to a sleeping Alycone to tell her that her husband had died.

The elm tree is described only by the Roman poet Virgil in his *Aeneid* as a place where dreams hid under each leaf.

This mysterious description is not developed, and so I decided in this tale to imagine the experiences of the tree: what it might have felt like to have those dreams hiding there, and to be standing so close to those grim walls. I also brought in Morpheus, another character shrouded in colourful mystery, in a brief entrance near the end. Morpheus has of course become well-known more recently through Neil Gaiman's *Sandman* series.

Holm Oak Tree

Acorns are the most charming nut of all the trees, with their smooth green shells, wrinkled like fingertips in a bath, and their delightful cups (called "cupules", an equally wonderful name). Depending on where you grew up, the acorns can look rounded and green, or brown and bulbous, or pointy, like the oak of the forthcoming tale, known as the holm oak.

I grew up with English oaks, their distinctive deep-lobed leaves, and huge thick-trunked trees. There are many beautiful oak species, but the holm oak is the one the Greeks and Romans most often wrote about. "Quercus ilex" is its scientific name. "Ilex" is the Latin word for "holly", and the holm oak's leaves are a lot like holly leaves, especially when new. They have spiky edges and are glossy, making them resilient to salty air when growing in coastal regions.

Holm oaks are evergreen trees, something which feels strange to someone who grew up with English oaks. They grow tall, up to twenty metres high. They are native to the Mediterranean, but they grow well in southern parts of Britain, where they are considered an invasive species.

The ancient Greeks used oak to make their ploughs - the ancient Greek writer Hesiod recommends oak as the best wood for their manufacture.

Acorns were said to be the food of the people who lived in the mythical first age of mankind, the so-called Golden Age. In later times, it was used mainly for animal feed, except for in times of famine.

The oak gets mentioned rather enigmatically by both Hesiod and Homer together with a "stone", and it is especially well-known as a tree sacred to Zeus, whose leaves' rustling was interpreted for tales of the future. And this brings us to our tale of the Holm Oak...

Holm Oak Tree

Quercus ilex
(HOLM OAK)

fig 1

fig 2

The Holm Oak's Tale

The whispering of tree leaves. People have always loved the sound. Though it doesn't sound like human voices speaking at all. It is not the way that we tree spirits talk either - our methods are far more secret than that, chemicals travelling through our sap, and into the earth below.

There is nothing quite like it, it is somewhere between a whisper and a rustle. Chattering, both without any words. As sudden and elusive as the breezes that cause our leaves to move. People have always come to listen to my leaves. Long, long, long ago, it was people walking alone, or couples, children come to hide, old friends come to sit. Now though, it is crowds, and I miss the old days.

My quiet life sheltering the occasional wanderers who came to sit by me changed quite suddenly one bright April morning. I had made it through another winter. My leaves are with me all year round, glossy against the greyness of those long months. By April, the rest of my world has become green again too, and the mornings are crisp, clear and full of new life. It was my favourite time of year, before I came to associate it with what happened that day.

I saw it coming through the white sky, a black dot that grew into the shape of a bird, and was headed straight for me.

Then, with a flurry of leaves, I felt its claws wrap around one of my branches. A black dove, its head pushing back and forth, looking here and there. It stayed there all morning, and though I didn't like the way it clutched so tightly on my branch, I didn't particularly sense anything else about it. Later, I heard the priestesses say that it had flowed all the way from Egypt, that mysterious land.

It wasn't until an elder from the village was walking by that I realised there was something quite unusual about this black bird in my branches. The old man was walking past, not intending to stop, as people often did, but when a voice emerged from my branches, he froze. I froze too. It was not a bird song or a sound any bird has ever made, but the voice of a human. A clear, young female voice.

The old man waited, clutching the cloth of his robe. I waited too. For a moment, just a gentle rustle of a couple of leaves in the faintest of spring breezes. But then the voice spoke again, clear as a bell.

"Lord Zeus, the thunderer, has chosen this tree for his oracle".

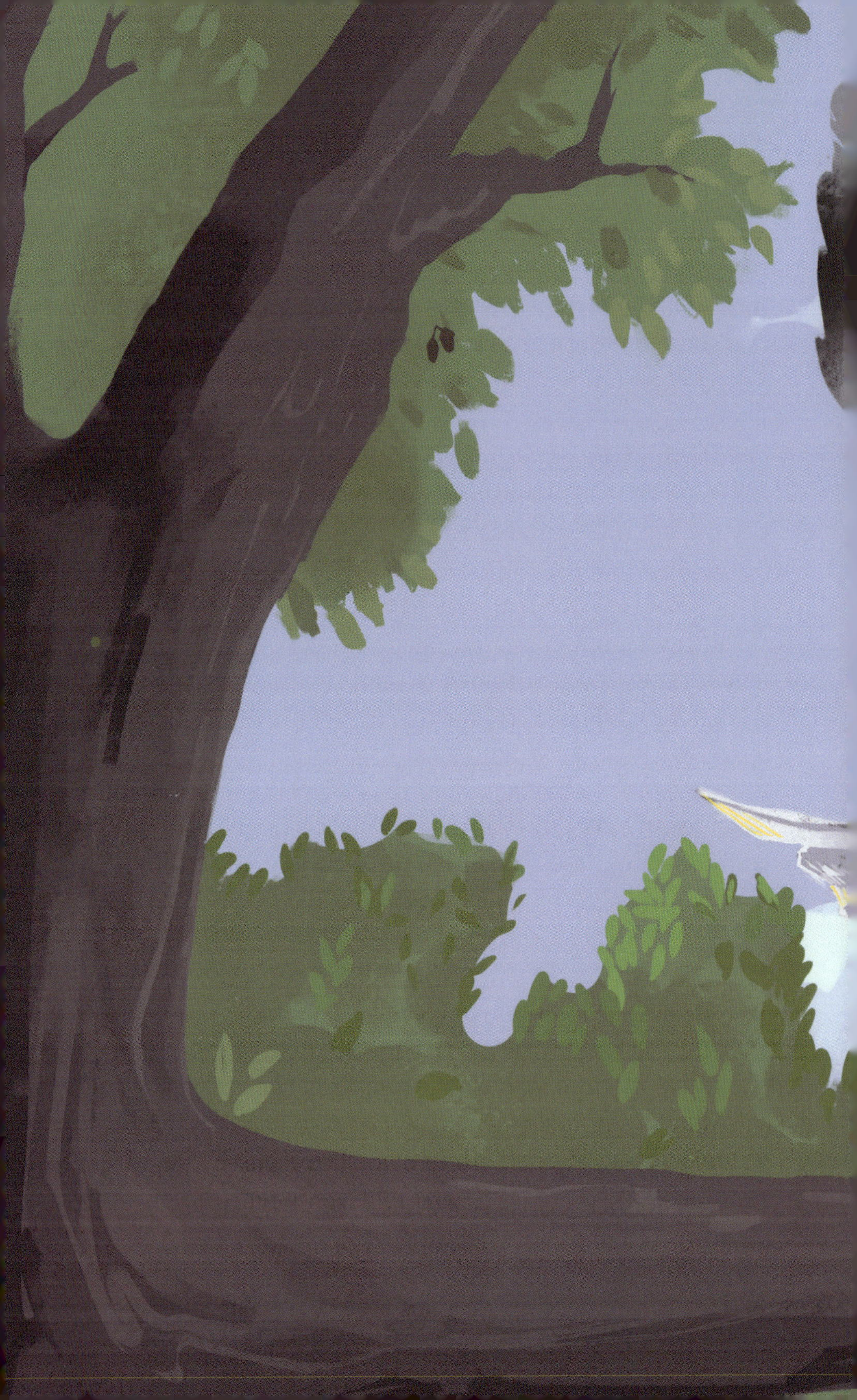

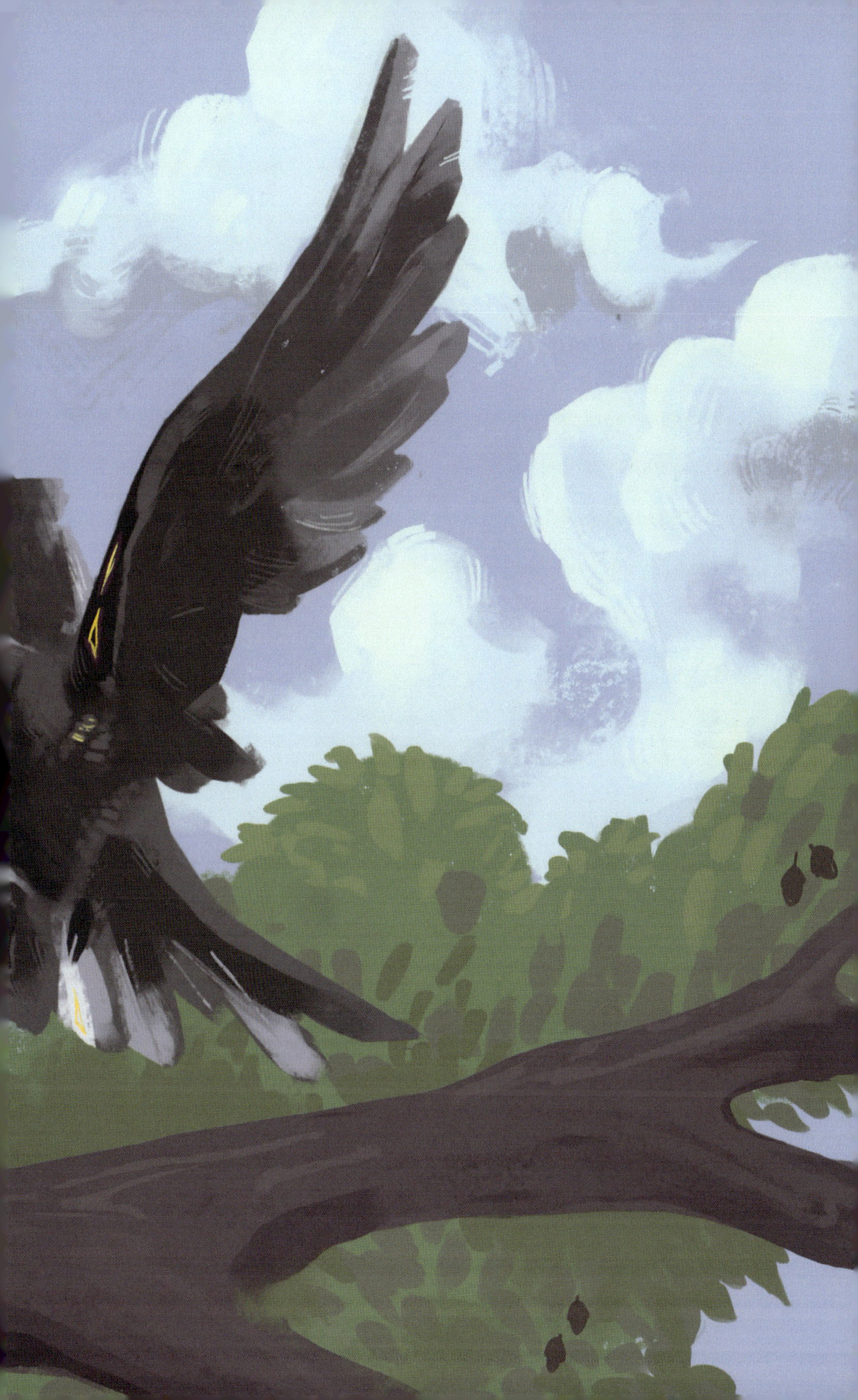

The man did not attempt to make conversation with the bird, but instead he hurried away. He looked frightened and I felt frightened too. This wasn't just going to go away.

The bird stayed among my branches, though she moved to a different branch from time to time. I was relieved each time, and her claws clutched hard and I could feel my skin being damaged.

By late afternoon, a crowd of local villagers had arrived, all talking seriously amongst themselves. They stared up into my branches at the bird, waiting.

The bird once again spoke with that eerie human voice:

"Lord Zeus, the thunderer, has chosen this tree for his oracle".

She repeated the statement three more times, and then, without warning, flapped her dark wings and was off, through a flurry of my leaves, and into the sky, rapidly becoming the dot I first saw that morning.

Everyone gasped and looked at one another in shock and uncertainty. No one knew what to do or say next, until a man I had never seen before, tall and forceful in his manner, announced: "we must obey Zeus. This tree will tell us the future."

"How will it do that?" someone called out, to a mumble of assent. "It's not like the tree speaks. Are we to look for signs in the acorns it litters the floor with in autumn, or the number of leaves that appear on each branch? Tell us a way of fulfilling the will of Zeus, for I cannot see one".

Everyone stood there for a while, and just at that point, an evening breeze swept under the leaves on my branches, and they rustled with a gentle chattering sound. The crowd looked at my leaves, expectantly, waiting for another breeze to set the leaves talking. It didn't come, though, as these evening breezes are fickle.

A lady stepped forward. "The tree speaks to us all the time!", she exclaimed. "We heard it just then". Her friend, standing near her, nodded in fervent agreement.

"What did it say?" said the loud man who had first spoken, looking at her incredulously. All eyes turned to the young woman. But she was as bold as her questioner.

"It told us that we should listen to the sound of the leaves!".

The crowd broke out into multiple discussions, a hubbub of noise that meant they all missed another breeze that set my glossy leaves chattering again. At last, the loud man declared: "These two women shall be the priestesses of this new oracle of Zeus the high thundering! Every day, they will come here to interpret the sound of the leaves."

The two women looked at each other, unsure of what to say, but the crowd was already joyfully declaring assent. That was how it all began.

It took awhile for word to spread. At first, the two women would arrive in the morning, with some bread and fruit to eat, and curious townspeople would visit and ask questions to my branches, like "who will my son marry?", "will I live a long life?", and similar things.

The women would attempt to interpret my leaves. It is hard to tell what they really felt or thought, as they didn't discuss it when they were sat under my branches, or walking through the orchard where my sisters grew. They talked about other things - the gossip of the town, arguments with their families and friends, things that annoyed them, things that they loved doing. I learned that one of the women loved the sound of the loom and the other preferred to be outdoors playing games with her younger brothers. I got to know who in the village they liked, and who they couldn't stand. I found out that the man with the loud voice was always taking charge and making decisions that angered others.

On windy days, there was too much chatter from my leaves to interpret it. It was a continuous stream. On days without wind, people made their journey for nothing. The women got fed up with themselves, and a new system needed to be put in place. Of course, my leaves were consulted about this new system. By this time, my acorns were scattered over the ground, and children would come to collect them in their clothing, and take them back home to boil and eat.

Lead tablets with carved signs started to be placed at my trunk instead, and there would be set days when the two women would appear to interpret the sound of my leaves. Clearly these women were getting something right, because within a few years the fame of the oracle of my leaves was spreading. Visitors would come from afar to place a tablet at my feet and wait patiently for their answers. All this time, the wind came and went, as it always does, sometimes blustering through my leaves, sending loose ones skittering along the ground, sometimes whispering gently through them. I never once knew what my leaves might be saying but the two women continued their messages.

We trees live far longer than humans, and the heart within me grew sad as I watched over time these women grow older. When one of them died from some sort of illness, there was a ceremony by my branches. The other woman was weeping silently for her friend, and the village uttered prayers of lament to Zeus. My leaves grow all year round, but around that time, I lost so many that I began to look like a tree that changes with the seasons.

Since that time, many women have been priestesses, listening to the wind in my leaves, and giving answers to the questions, but I have never forgotten the first two who spent those years beside me, listening to the rustling. In all that time, the truth of it all has remained a mystery.

Notes

The fifth century BC Greek historian Herodotus is the source for this story of how there came to be an oracle at Dodona. There is some debate about how the oak tree was used: was it the rustling of the leaves or something hanging from the tree? I wrote this version because I was interested in the idea that the tree itself does not know if there is any truth in anything that is being interpreted. I also wanted to capture the dramatic moment of the speaking dove arriving, and how that might have led to the oracle being established.

The poet Apollonius of Rhodes imagined that the Argo, famed boat in the story of the Argonauts, had been made from oak from Dodona and therefore could speak the future. I thought about including this, but wanted to keep my story within the forest setting.

Black Poplar Tree

These trees are now rare in Britain, which makes their triangular, heart-like, serrated leaves, and dark, rugged bark seem even more precious a find. I am lucky to have discovered a black poplar growing right around the corner. It had been standing in its solitary glory, with a fire of yellow leaves in autumn, for many years before I identified it. Its knobbly bark stands out against the sky.

The branches are curved, and good therefore for supporting buildings, and their shoots are sturdy and are said to have been used in Victorian times for clothes pegs. They grow in moist, low-lying regions, and can reach up to 30 metres.

It produces a red blossom, and lots of seed wool which creates the appearance of snow when it floats and falls. They are part of the willow family, a tree associated with sadness in the minds of many through the much-loved Weeping Willow. The story of the Black Poplar below is one of mourning.

In another source of sadness, its decline greatly troubles environmentalists, as the tree makes a home for many species of insect and moth, as well as the butterflies Large Tortoiseshell and Camberwell beauty. Draining of the soil and competing imported trees have led to a dramatic drop in numbers of these elegantly leaning trees with their curving branches.

The Black Poplar was well-known to the ancient Greeks and Romans. The ancient Greek doctor Galen described the use of a cream made from its buds which he thought reduced inflammation, a use which still continues today in popular "Poplar Buds" creams. As it is part of the willow family, its bark contains salicin, which is the acid that forms the basis for that well-known painkiller, aspirin.

As the twigs start to grow in spring, there are little amber drops at the end of each one. These golden droplets, as well as decorating the trees with glowing dots throughout their branches, are also turned into resin by bees and used to construct their hives.

These drops of resin feature in the story below in quite a different way.

Black Poplar's Tale

I remember him best as a small child these days, throwing acorns at our heads, and grinning when they landed on our noses and foreheads. He had a mop of tawny hair, and soft brown eyes, the colour of dark honey. He was happy then. We seven sisters were older than him by several years, and we probably spoiled him and plagued him with our sisterly jibes, advice and worries.

He liked to explore, and as he got bigger, he outgrew the woods and the river by our little house, and would disappear for the day, coming back with scratches, and bruises, and a mouth stained with berries he had eaten from trees and bushes as he journeyed.

We would chide him and patch up his wounds, using poplar bark to soothe them. "Where have you been?" one of my sisters, usually Merope, would ask. She was the strictest of us all. He would sometimes shrug, but at other times he would tell us where he had been. He spoke of villages, passers-by with walking sticks and stories, trees and plants we had never seen before.

My water-loving sisters and I preferred to stay by our woodland home, tending to our garden, watching the river eddy by. We did not share his adventuring spirit, but we loved to hear his tales.

Over the years, he grew leaner and longer. His boyish cheeks became sculpted with cheek bones, and the grin, though still recognisable, was less childlike. We no doubt changed too, but less so, as we were already nearly fully grown when he was born. He really did feel like our child in some ways.

One day he came home from the local town where he sat with some other boys and learned about the world, about how to make armour, how to count and how to read the stars, from an old, wise man who taught them in exchange for bowls of apples and walnuts, acorns and berries.

He said nothing as he came through our door, and was silent for most of the evening. Aegle gently asked him: "has something happened?"

He remained silent for a few moments, but then it began to pour out, that release of a painful story that one has been holding inside, causing unseen damage. A boy had told him that our father was not really our father at all. He had responded angrily, but the words had planted doubt in his mind.

"Don't listen to this unkind, jealous boy!" we said. "Of course our father is our true father. Do you not see him shining on our house every day?"

"That's not enough, though. I have to hear it from him".

We all looked at each other uncomfortably. He was a great adventurer, but this was a journey it was unwise for anyone to make. It was a long way, and we had not spoken to our father either. Our mother had told us who he was, but we did not know how he would react to see his son in his court.

"Just forget about it" Dioxippe urged him, as the rest of us cleared the dinner bowls, and murmured amongst ourselves.

But of course he didn't forget about it. It wasn't in his nature. He always was an explorer, and investigator, one who went on quests, and wanted answers. Within a week, he had packed his bags, hugged us all farewell, and set off. There was no stopping him.

Some weeks went by, and we heard nothing. Of course, we would not always expect to hear things, but word travelled fast even back then, without all the devices that make everyone connected. We talked amongst ourselves at dinner, and looked anxiously up at the sky on bright sunny days.

Then strange conditions started to appear. Day and night became disordered at first, moving far more quickly than it should. We remarked to each other on the speed at which the day passed. Twilight set in sooner, and we found that our usual daily tasks were unfinished.

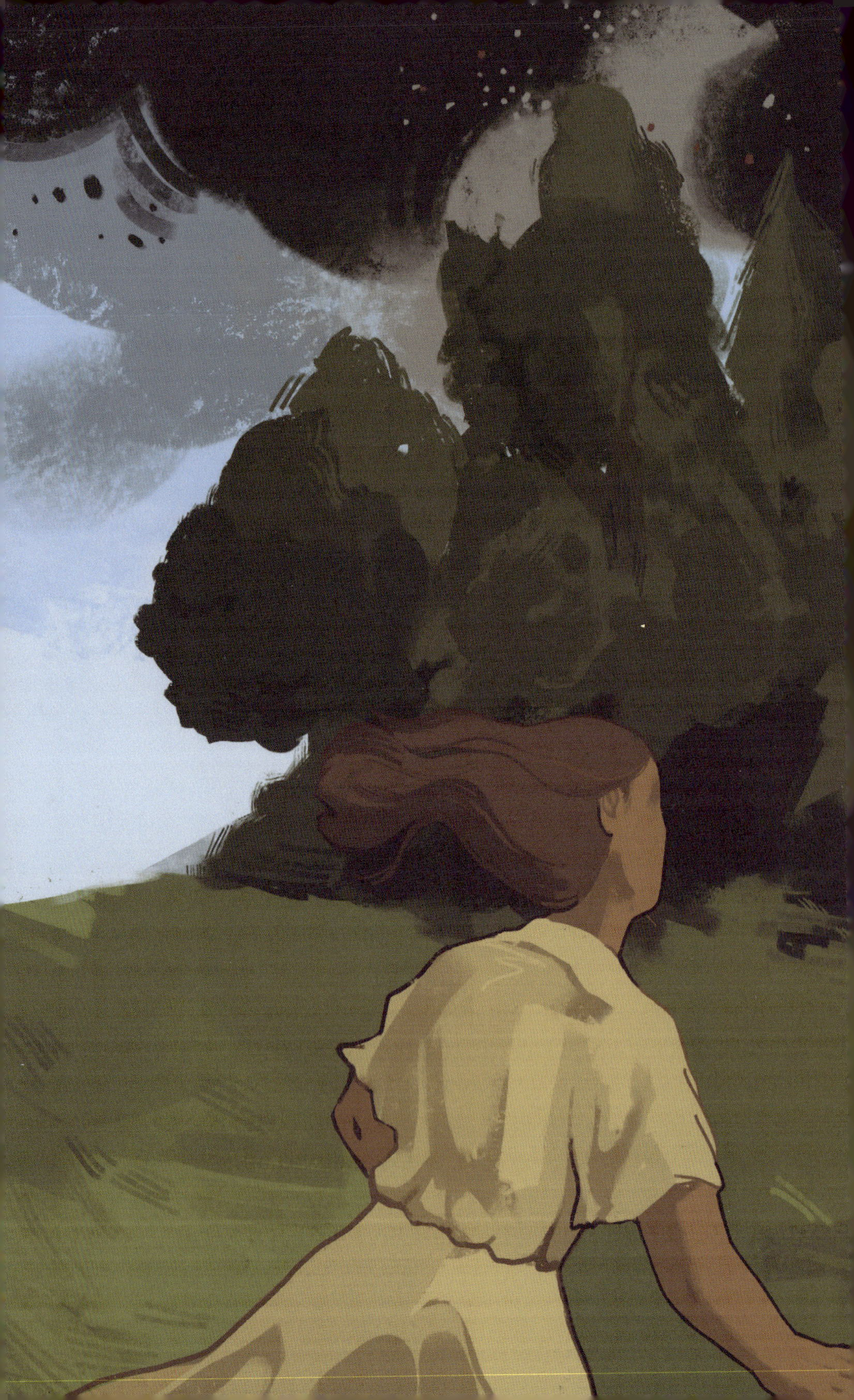

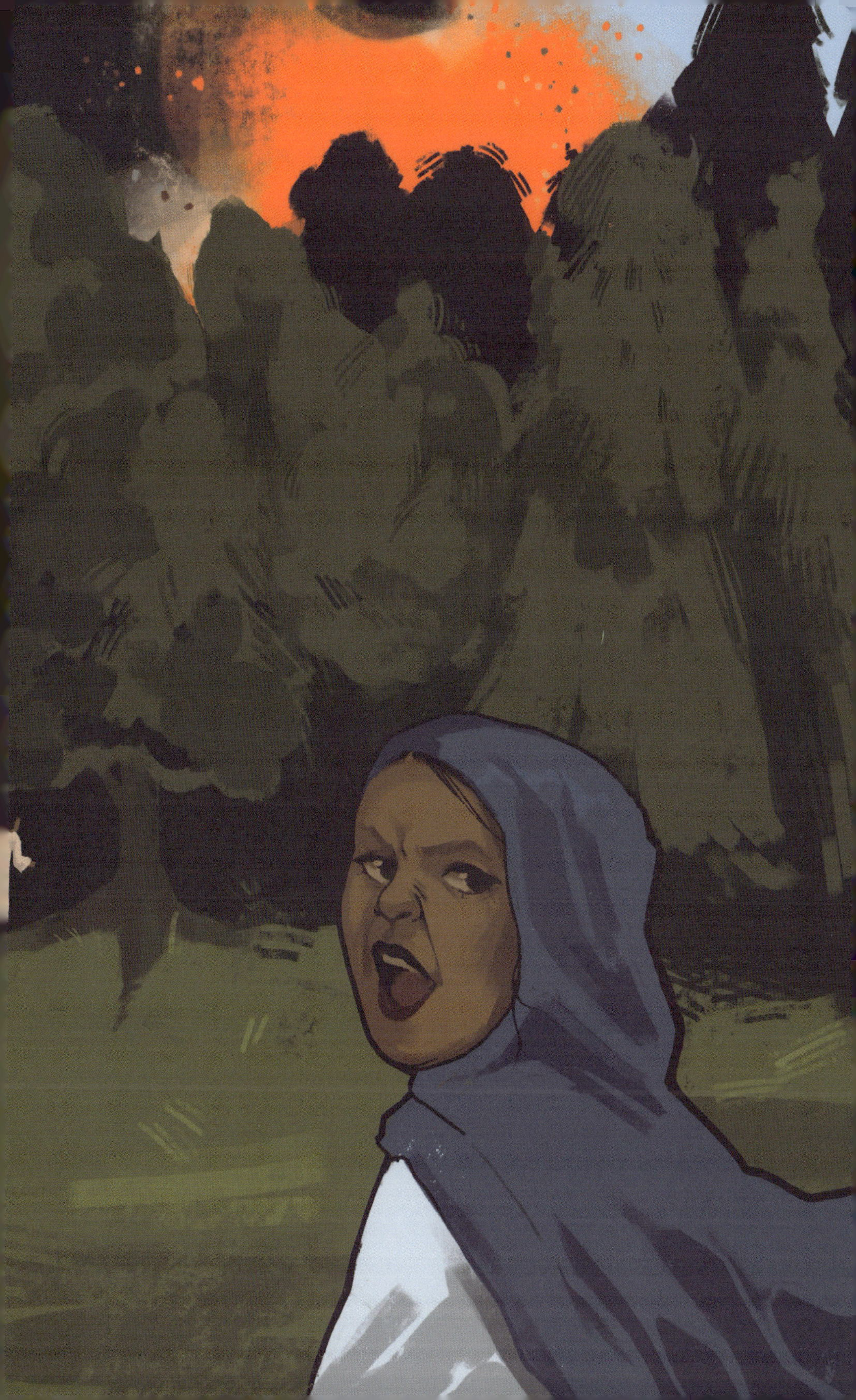

"Is it an omen?" asked Lampetie, anxiously.

"Don't be silly!" said Merope, a little too hastily. But that was only the beginning of the strangeness of those times.

We woke up one morning, after an unsatisfyingly short sleep, to discover our beloved river was frozen, with little birds padding their feet over its icy surface, and the trees clinked and sparkled with a wintry frost.

"How can this happen in the middle of spring?" I exclaimed. No one answered, but all of us glanced up at the sun, so pale and far away through the cold skies. The next day, we woke to the opposite. Our river was parched, and our wood smelled of flames. We ran through the trees looking for the source of the fire. It took a little while but it was Helie who found it first, and called out to us in shock.

There was our dear brother, lying on the ground, his skin smouldering, and his face turned down in the mud. Merope pulled his head up, and one by one we sat by his body, touching the hot skin. He was already dead. There was nothing we could do but sit beside his poor, burned body.

Later, we heard all sorts of stories about what had happened: that he'd asked for the chariot of our father, that those strong, fierce, powerful horses ran wild without the might of our father's arms holding their reins, and how the whole world was scorched and frozen until he was struck out of the sky by lightning.

Of course there were other stories too. Some even blamed us and claimed we had encouraged him, and even helped him steal the chariot. The ugliest tales begin to grow around tragedies.

But for those days and weeks, we knew nothing other than our brother, that joyful, mischievous boy we had known all his life, was gone. After three days of watching, we buried his body in a small ceremony with a jar of oil, and a few of his childhood toys. All seven of us wept that day, tears that never seemed to stop falling.

It seemed from that moment that we found him that we never stopped weeping. No amount of mourning could ease the loss, so there we spent our days.

Over time, we started to feel our bodies changing, the flesh stiffening, and the skin deeping and furrowing and darkening. Instead of veins full of rushing blood, sap filled our bodies, sticky and slow. The golden drops were just the same colour as his eyes when they caught the sun. They fell into the river below, whose current took them away downstream, venturing where we never chose to. Just as we always had done, we stayed by our river and our wood, seven sisters, and we carried on filling the river with our honey-like tear drops.

Sometimes people come walking through the wood, under our dark old branches, seven black poplars with their big burrs, and they stop and look at the stone where we carved his name:

PHAETHON.

Notes

This story is told by the Roman poet in his *Metamorphoses*. There, the changing, grieving sisters are a brief addendum, whereas Phaethon's journey is centre stage, so in this retelling, I wanted to foreground the sisters' story. They don't actually appear until the end of the story in Ovid so their grief feels rather overblown and out of place, like people grieving a famous person, but it struck me that they would have grown up with Phaethon, so it was this element I chose to explore.

There are lots of stories of people turning into trees in Ovid's wonderful poem, but the way in which the story fits the phases of the tree, with its sparkling buds of resin, and its love of water meadows, is particularly beautiful.

Printed in Great Britain
by Amazon